TEEN TITA

BRAIN SWAP

By Devan Aptekar
Illustrated by Jason Armstrong
Color by Lee Loughridge

© 2006 DC Comics.
TEEN TITANS and all related characters and elements are trademarks of DC Comics © 2006.
All rights reserved.

Published by Scholastic Inc. SCHOLASTIC and associated logos are
trademarks and/or registered trademarks of Scholastic. Inc.

ISBN 0-439-83009-5

12 11 10 9 8 7 6 5 4 3 2 1   6 7 8 9 10/0

Printed in the U.S.A.
First printing, November 2006

SCHOLASTIC INC.

New York Toronto London Auckland Sydney

Mexico City New Delhi Hong Kong Buenos Aires

In his secret underground theater, the Puppet King was getting restless. His wooden toys had gotten tiresome. He had practiced long enough.

It was time to capture the real thing.

"Azarath . . . Metrion . . . Zinthos," Raven chanted as she meditated. It was late afternoon, and Raven thought she had found some peace and quiet.

She was wrong.

"Please forgive me for bothering you, Raven," said Starfire. "Have you seen Robin?"

"No," Raven said, hoping Starfire would leave.

"Perhaps you have seen Cyborg?" asked Starfire.

"I'm trying to meditate," groaned Raven. "I haven't seen anyone."

"They must be doing the 'hanging out' somewhere," said Starfire. She gave Raven a hopeful smile. "Perhaps *we* should do the 'hanging out'? We might journey to the mall of shopping or—"

Raven opened her eyes to glare at Starfire. She hated being interrupted during her meditation.

Raven took a deep breath and ignored Starfire's voice. "Azarath . . . Metrion . . . Zin—" she began.

"MAIL CALL!" shouted Cyborg as he entered the room. He was holding a big package.

"Check it out," said Beast Boy. "There was some fan mail left by the front door."

They unwrapped the box and found five Teen Titan puppets inside.

"Aw, isn't that cute," said Cyborg. "Puppet Cy has a light-up eye."

Beast Boy attacked Robin's puppet. "Hey, dude," taunted Beast Boy, "my puppet is totally kicking your puppet's butt!"

"Not for long," yelled Robin.

"Raven, shall my tiny replica do battle with your tiny replica?" asked Starfire.

Raven handed her puppet to Starfire and sighed. "Knock yourself out," said Raven.

That night, however, there was another surprise in store for the Titans. The Puppet King crept out of the large box's hidden compartment. He activated his remote control. It began to glow.

The sleeping Titans were pulled out of their bodies and into the puppets. Raven was awake meditating, and Starfire was patrolling the hallways, so they were spared.

"Raven, have you also heard the strange noises?" asked Starfire.

"The strange noises of you talking right outside my door?" asked Raven. "Kind of hard to miss."

Suddenly, Robin, Cyborg, and Beast Boy attacked Raven and Starfire. The girls dove out of the way.

"Robin!" cried Starfire. "I do not understand. Stop!"

"Beast Boy, it's me," yelled Raven. "Don't make me hurt you."

"Friends, why do you attack us?" asked Starfire.

The Puppet King chuckled. "Oh, they're not your friends anymore," he said. "They are my puppets. *These* are your friends!" He raised up the little wooden puppets of Robin, Cyborg, and Beast Boy.

The puppets' voices were muffled, but both Starfire and Raven recognized them. The Puppet King was telling the truth.

"Release them!" commanded Raven.

"Sorry, you don't command *me*," snarled the Puppet King. "I command *you*. With the Puppet King pulling the strings, the Teen Titans will command the entire city!"

He raised his magical control. Raven and Starfire felt their energies being torn from their bodies.

Raven gathered herself together. "Azarath . . . Metrion
. . . Zinthos!" she shouted with her last breath.

The Puppet King was knocked backward. "My control!"
he shouted, scrambling after the remote.

Raven and Starfire turned and ran. They hadn't yet
noticed the huge change that had just occurred.

Raven and Starfire stopped and stared at each other in shock. They were looking at themselves!

Raven saw she was in Starfire's body.

And Starfire saw she was in Raven's body.

"Raven!" yelled Starfire. "You are me! And I am you! This is awful!"

A nearby parking meter melted. A mailbox exploded. "Starfire," said Raven urgently. "You have to calm down. My powers are driven by emotion. The more you feel, the more energy you'll unleash."

"It's Beast Boy!" shouted Starfire.

"You mean *Puppet* Beast Boy," said Raven. She grabbed Starfire and tried to launch into the air with her, but couldn't. "Okay, how do you fly this thing?" she asked Starfire.

"You must feel the unbridled joy of flight," said Starfire.

"Unbridled joy? Not really my thing," Raven said, biting her lip. "What do I have to feel to use star bolts?"

"Righteous fury!" said Starfire with passion.

"Your alien strength?" asked Raven hesitantly.

"Boundless confidence!" announced Starfire.

Raven groaned.

Soon Robin and Cyborg arrived.

Raven grabbed Starfire's shoulders. "If I can't fly, you have to levitate," she said urgently. "You know those words I always—"

"YES!" exclaimed Starfire. She closed her eyes and took a deep breath. "Azarath . . . Metrion . . . Zinthos!"

Starfire and Raven rose into the air. At first, Starfire was excited, but as they spun, she began to get scared.

"I wish to stop!" she cried. "Please tell me the way to stop!"

"Look at the ground and imagine—WAIT!"

Starfire had looked at the ground too soon. The two Titans were falling fast.

They landed safely in a pile of trash.

"Our friends are in danger!" said Starfire. "We must follow and—"

"And what?" demanded Raven. "Save them with my unusable powers and your unbridled emotions?"

"On my planet, even a newborn can unleash the joy of flight," said Starfire hotly. "But you are too busy being grumpy and rude to feel anything at all!"

"Maybe you haven't noticed, but my emotions are dangerous," snapped Raven. "I can't afford to feel anything!"

Raven turned away from Starfire. "You may have my body, but you don't know anything about me."

"Perhaps you are right," said Starfire, smiling. "If you and I are to overcome this, we must know everything about each other. So start sharing."

Raven gave her a small smile in return. "Okay. I was born on Azarath."

The two Teen Titans told each other about their lives as they tracked their friends back to the Puppet King's lair.

By the end of their journey, Raven was even able to fly! And Starfire had learned how to control Raven's powers better. They were ready to save their friends.

Starfire and Raven burst into the Puppet King's lair just in time. The Puppet King was about to destroy the puppets—with their friends' spirits trapped inside!

Unfortunately, they had to fight their friends' bodies to get to the Puppet King.

Raven soared through the air, battling Robin. She was unable to shoot star bolts at him. She just couldn't feel enough righteous fury toward Robin, even though she knew the Puppet King was controlling her friend.

But when she turned to face the Puppet King himself, Raven couldn't take it anymore. Star bolts shot from her hands, knocking him down. His precious control flew into the magical flames of his cauldron.

As the control burned in the flames, the Teen Titans felt themselves being pulled back into their bodies.

"My remote control!" screamed the Puppet King. "The magic! Without it, I'm just a . . . " he shuddered and fell to the floor, turning back into a puppet.

"I am me!" Starfire said to Raven. "And you are you!"
"And we're us!" added Cyborg happily.
"Thanks to you two," said Robin.
"You go, girls!" cheered Beast Boy.

"Raven, we have done it!" shouted Starfire, wrapping her arms around Raven joyously.

"Okay—you're hugging me," said Raven.

The next day, Starfire interrupted Raven's meditation and asked if she could join her.

Together they chanted, "Azarath . . . Metrion . . . Zinthos."

"Starfire?" asked Raven, opening one eye. "After this, would you like to go to the mall?"

"Yes!" Starfire said happily.